Stanley the Sock Monster Goes to the Moon

little bee books

An imprint of Bonnier Publishing Group

853 Broadway, New York, New York 10003

Copyright © 2013 by Jedda Robaard.

First published by The Five Mile Press 2013. This little bee books edition 2015.

All rights reserved, including the right of reproduction in whole or in part in any form.

LITTLE BEE BOOKS is a trademark of Bonnier Publishing Group, and associated

colophon is a trademark of Bonnier Publishing Group.

Manufactured in China 1014 LEO

First Edition 2 4 6 8 10 9 7 5 3 1

Library of Congress Control Number: 2014943632

ISBN 978-1-4998-0012-8

www.littlebeebooks.com

www.bonnierpublishing.com

By Jedda Robaard

Stanley the Sock Monster Goes to the Moon

little bee books

Every night, Dad would read Stanley his favorite book.

Stanley really, really wanted to go to the moon.

"You can go anywhere you imagine, Stanley,"
his dad would say.

One night, Stanley decided it was time for a plan.

He gathered all his space books, notes, and sketches.

First, Stanley decided to try his moonboot.

He waited and waited for it to take off...

but nothing happened!

Then he thought he could hitch a ride on a shooting star...

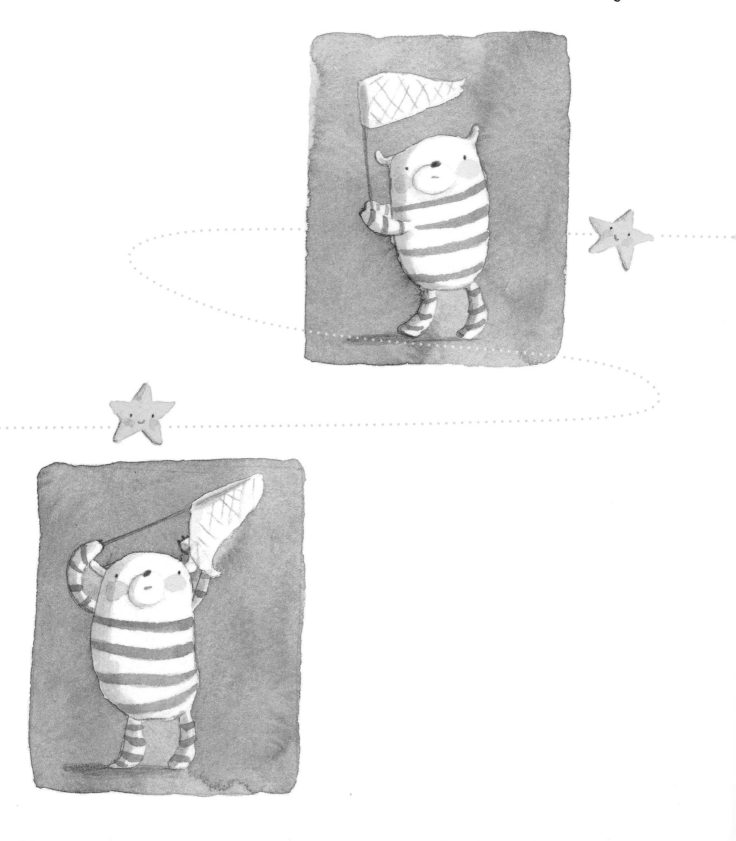

but Stanley couldn't
catch one.

His
mouse
friend
said
that
the
moon
was
made
of
cheese...

but Mouse had never been there.

Stanley asked the cow who jumped over the moon...

but she wasn't very helpful at all.

Sometimes Stanley thought that the moon
looked very large and very close...

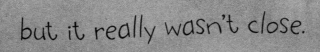

but it really wasn't close.

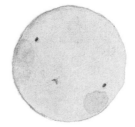

Stanley didn't think he was ever going to reach the moon.

His dad told him to look at it another way...

When suddenly, the answer came to him.

Finally,

he made a rocket...

and launch day soon arrived.

Stanley asked his dad to help him start the countdown.

5, 4, 3, 2, 1...

Off he went!

It was just as wonderful as Stanley had always imagined.

And when he returned,
Stanley brought back
the stars...

and shared them
  with everyone.